NAILED IT!

Extreme CLIFF DIVING

Virginia Loh-Hagan

45th Parallel Press

Published in the United States of America by Cherry Lake Publishing
Ann Arbor, Michigan
www.cherrylakepublishing.com

Content Adviser: Liv Williams, Editor, www.iLivExtreme.com
Reading Adviser: Marla Conn, ReadAbility, Inc.
Photo Credits: ©Dean Treml/Red Bull Content Pool, 5; ©Paulo Calisto/Red Bull Content Pool, 6; ©Romina Amato/Red Bull Content Pool, 8; ©Romina Amato/Red Bull Content Pool, 11; ©Action Images/ZUMAPRESS/Newscom, 13; ©Ray Demski/ Red Bull Content Pool, 15; ©Dean Treml/Red Bull Content Pool, 17; ©Tomislav Moze/Red Bull Content Pool, 19; ©Romina Amato/Red Bull Content Pool, 21; ©Gary Hartz/Dreamstime.com, 23; ©Romina Amato/Red Bull Content Pool, 24; ©robcocquyt/shutterstock.com, 27; ©Duncan Soar /Alamy Stock Photo, 29; ©Trusjom/Shutterstock.com, multiple interior pages; ©Kues/Shutterstock.com, multiple interior pages

45th Parallel Press is an imprint of Cherry Lake Publishing.

Library of Congress Cataloging-in-Publication Data

Names: Loh-Hagan, Virginia.
Title: Extreme cliff diving / by Virginia Loh-Hagan.
Description: Ann Arbor : Cherry Lake Publishing, [2016] | Series: Nailed it! | Includes bibliographical references and index.
Identifiers: LCCN 2015049729| ISBN 9781634710893 (hardcover) | ISBN 9781634711883 (pdf) | ISBN 9781634712873 (paperback) | ISBN 9781634713863 (ebook)
Subjects: LCSH: Cliff diving--Juvenile literature. | Extreme sports--Juvenile literature.
Classification: LCC GV838.67.C55 L65 2016 | DDC 797.2--dc23
LC record available at http://lccn.loc.gov/2015049729

Printed in the United States of America
Corporate Graphics Inc.

ABOUT THE AUTHOR

Dr. Virginia Loh-Hagan is an author, university professor, former classroom teacher, and curriculum designer. Instead of diving off cliffs, she likes diving into cheese dips. She lives in San Diego with her very tall husband and very naughty dogs.

Table of Contents

1

Diving Heroes

Who are some famous cliff divers? What makes them special?

Ginger Huber went to the end of the cliff. She took a deep breath. She relaxed her shoulders. She trusted herself. She knew what she was doing.

She didn't have time to count to three. She didn't want to change her mind. She dived. Her rear end faced the water. She couldn't see the water. Most female cliff divers won't do this move.

It's called the Flying Front. She won awards for it. She competes in the Red Bull Cliff Diving World Series.

She trains. She needs high cliffs. She has to drive to faraway places. She finds a way.

Laso Schaller jumped from a 193-foot (59 meters) cliff. He leaned forward a little. He tensed his body. He folded his hands. His hands were in front of his hips. He dived. He braced for the **impact** on his face. Impact means to hit something hard. He went over 75 miles (121 kilometers) an hour. He was in the air for 3.58 seconds.

The World High Diving Federation requires scuba divers to be present for dives over 65 feet (20 m) high.

Hitting the water can sound like a gunshot.

He overshot his landing. He was underwater for a couple of seconds. He came up. He swam to shore. The landing pulled out his right leg. He dislocated his right hip. But he smiled. And he kept on cliff diving.

Steven LoBue jumped from 89 feet (27 m) in the air. He jumped from a **platform** built on a cliff. A platform is like a diving board. He didn't dive out far enough. His head hit the platform.

That didn't stop him. He continued with his dive. He did a back triple **somersault**. A somersault is like a flip.

NAILED IT!

Spotlight Biography: Orlando Duque

Orlando Duque is "The Duke" of cliff diving. He's won 11 world titles. He has two world records. He's from Colombia. He started at age nine. First, he dived in swimming pools. He did Olympic-style diving. But he grew tired of pools. He needed more of a challenge. So he dived off cliffs. He said, "When I'm standing up on top, I'm worried. I know this is high. It's going to be some danger involved in the dive. But I still want to do it. ... In three seconds you went from being really worried and now you're in the water and you're super happy. It just changes really quickly and it's hard to compare to anything else." Duque has been cliff diving for over 20 years. He said, "Every year is getting better in terms of diving, also the sport is growing." He'd like cliff diving to be an Olympic sport.

Spectators are audience members. They like watching cliff divers.

He did four twists. He landed feetfirst. He said, "I finished the whole dive. So I was happy about that."

He had a huge cut. The cut was above his left eye. He said, "I think that just got the best of me a little bit. But, I made it down to the water safely."

2

Daring Diving

What is cliff diving? How is cliff diving different from platform diving? What do cliff divers need?

Cliff diving is a **precision** sport. Cliff divers need to have perfect timing. They study the cliffs. They study **obstacles**, or objects. They study water depths. They study tides. They calculate distances. They study the angle and speed of hitting water. One mistake means injury or death.

Cliff diving is a type of high diving. High diving is jumping from great heights. Cliff diving is more dangerous. Cliff divers jump from high cliffs. They dive fast. They dive into water. They don't make a big splash.

Their flight is about three seconds long. Things happen quickly for cliff divers.

Cliff diving is different from Olympic platform diving. Platform divers jump from a diving board. Cliff divers jump from cliffs. Platform divers jump from about 32 feet (9.75 m). They hit the water at about 30 miles (48 km) per hour. Cliff divers jump from at least 60 feet (18 m). They hit the water at over 60 miles (96.5 km) per hour. They hit the water with nine times more force.

Cliff diving is an adventure sport. It has a high level of danger. It involves speed and height.

Extreme Cliff Diving: Know the Lingo

Back group: jumping off and rotating backward

Barani: somersault combined with half-twist

Blind entry: diving with the rear end first

Flying: somersault in the straight position and then a tuck or pike

Free: dives that involve twists with straight, pike, and tuck positions

Front group: jumping off and rotating forward

Inward group: jumping off backward and then rotating forward

Pike: flight position with legs sticking out

Reverse group: jumping while facing the water and then rotating backward

Straight: flight position with no bend in the hips or knees

Tuck: flight position with the body folded up in a tight ball

Twist group: twisting or rotating while diving

Platform diving is featured in the Olympics.

Platform divers land with their hands first. Cliff divers land feetfirst. They dive from extreme heights. They don't want other body parts to hit first. Bodies can't handle multiple impacts. Cliff divers press their legs together. They use all their strength.

The **aerial** aspects are similar. Aerial means happening in the air. Divers do flips. They do twists.

Cliff diving is a simple extreme sport. There's no special gear. But cliff divers wear formfitting suits. They don't wear normal swimming clothes. The extra fabric creates **drag**. Drag is a pulling feeling. The drag forces legs apart. This could cause injuries.

Cliff diving is dangerous. It requires special skills. Cliff divers are highly trained. They start by diving in pools. Then they increase the heights of their dives.

Orlando Duque is a cliff diver. He said, "The most important thing in our sport is the leg muscles." He does a lot of one-legged squats.

Cliff divers have control of their bodies and minds.

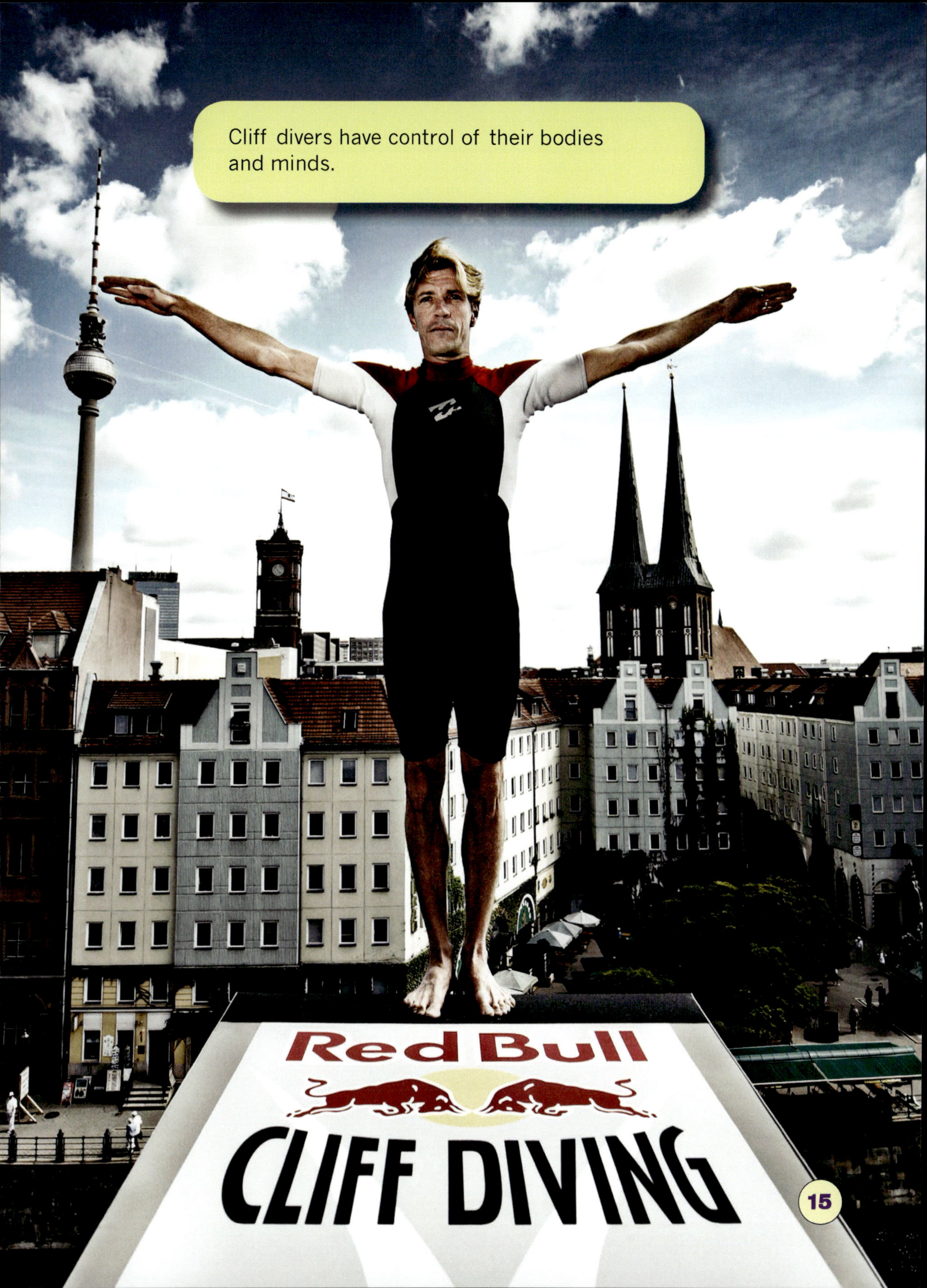

3

Diving Dangers

What are the dangers cliff drivers need to think about? What are some things cliff divers can do to ensure their safety?

Matt Heffernan jumped off a 60-foot (18 m) cliff. The cliff was called "King Kong." It's in Utah. He tried to do a double backflip. He landed on his face. He sank to the bottom. He died.

Cliff diving can cause injury or death. Cliff divers prepare for danger. They check the cliffs. They check the landing space. They make sure no swimmers are in the water. Cliff divers don't want to land on anybody.

Jumping from cliffs increases pressure. This can blow out eardrums. It is very painful. Cliff divers need to take care of their ears. They put drops of olive oil in their ears.

Cliff divers travel at extreme speeds for a short period of time. Impact can be dangerous. Water is not a cushion. It feels like concrete. It can feel like a car accident. It can compress spines. It can break bones.

Cliff divers should never dive alone.

Cliff divers need to land straight as a pencil. Misplaced hands could break wrists. Slight tilts could hurt body organs. Chins sticking out could bruise faces.

NAILED IT!

Advice from the Field: Rachelle "Rocco" Simpson

Rachelle "Rocco" Simpson is America's queen of cliff diving. She's the first female champion of the Red Bull Cliff Diving World Series. She jumps from 65 feet (20 m). She twists. She somersaults. She slams into the water at high speed. She enters the water feetfirst. She gets scared every time she dives. Her advice is to stay calm. She said, "To be a high diver, you need to be able to keep mentally calm. When you're getting amped up, that's when you can really mess up. You need to be able to overcome your fear." She tries not to overthink things. She remembers that she's done hundreds of dives. She practices. She does gymnastics.

Cliff divers need to form a 90-degree angle with the water when they land.

Landing on your rear end could chip teeth.

Cliff divers could get blown sideways. They could hit rocks. They could get knocked out. They could die.

Cliff divers stretch their toes. They keep their arms tight to their sides. They jump with a straight, tight body. They blow hard out of their noses. They keep their mouths closed tight.

The water can be dangerous. **Currents** are strong flows of water. They could pull cliff divers under.

The water could be **polluted**. There could be poisons in the water. Cliff divers could get sick. They could get infected. Cliff divers shouldn't dive if they have open cuts. Cliff divers don't want water in their noses or mouths. They push their breath out of their noses. This keeps water from getting in.

Some water is **murky**. It's not clear. Cliff divers can't see obstacles. They could hit rocks.

Cliff divers do their tricks early in the dive. Then they prepare their bodies. They get in proper positions to hit the water.

Choppy waters and high waves hide the surface of the water. This affects cliff divers' entry.

4 Developing Cliff Diving

Where did cliff diving start? Who helped develop cliff diving as a sport?

Cliff diving started in the late 1700s. It started in Hawaii. King Kahekili jumped off a 70-foot (21 m) cliff. He jumped into **sacred** waters. Sacred means special. He became known as "Birdman." He set an example for his warriors. His warriors jumped. They proved their bravery. They proved their loyalty.

Later, King Kamehameha perfected lele kawa. This means jumping feetfirst without making a splash. Locals began cliff diving. He turned cliff diving into a competition. He judged the style of the dive. He judged the amount of splash.

In 1934, Enrique Apac Rios jumped from La Quebrada. It's in Acapulco, Mexico. Rios was 13. He inspired the La Quebrada cliff divers. They're professional cliff divers. They dive 115 feet (35 m) into the sea.

The World High Diving Federation promoted cliff diving. It organizes competitions. It created guidelines for judging.

Cliff diving started on Maui and Easter Island.

Cliff divers get more points for more difficult moves and for clean takeoffs and entries.

Officials judge the **takeoff**. This is when cliff divers jump off. They judge the tricks done in the air. They judge somersaults and twists. They judge positions in the air. They judge entry into the water.

Red Bull hosts the Cliff Diving World Series. It established this competition in 2009. Cliff divers participate in several events. They jump from platforms 85 to 92 feet (26 to 28 m) high. The champion scores the highest number of points. This competition made cliff diving popular.

NAILED IT!

That Happened?!?

Titti is a Jack Russell terrier. She lives in Malta. The dog dives from 12-foot-high (3.6 m) cliffs. She dives at the same time as her owner. Her owner is Carmelo Abela. They perform together a lot. They leap together. Then they swim together. Abela said, "She trusts me. And whatever I do, she does it. When I tell her to jump, she jumps. But if anyone else tries to jump with her, she won't. She just trusts me." Their bond is incredible. Abela taught Titti to dive and swim at four months old. He started her at smaller heights. Titti was scared at first. But now she shows no fear. Abela said, "When we arrive she is anxious ... she wants to dive. She's amazing. She is crazy about jumping."

5

Future of Cliff Diving

What is rope jumping? Why do people want to ban cliff diving?

Extreme cliff divers are always looking for new challenges. They developed rope jumping. Rope jumping combines cliff diving and rock climbing.

Rope jumpers jump from cliffs. But they use ropes. These ropes don't bounce. This makes divers come to a stop at the end of their fall. It's dangerous.

Toby Benham was an Australian **daredevil**. Daredevils do daring stunts. He was also a circus performer. He almost died twice. He called himself "Lucky Chance." Once he had a cliff jump go wrong. He broke his hip. His lung collapsed. He was in a coma. But he lived.

Then he rope jumped. The cliff he was on is called "Death Swing." Benham smashed into sharp rocks. He died.

Cliff diving is also known as tombstoning. A **tombstone** is a large, flat stone. It marks a grave. Cliff divers dive straight like tombstones. Cliff diving is known to be deadly.

Cliff divers look for ways to make their sport more extreme.

Sunset Cliffs is in San Diego, California. The Arch is a popular jumping spot. Young daredevils run. Then they

NAILED IT!

When Extreme Is Too Extreme!

Imagine cliff diving with ghosts! Waimea Falls is in Hawaii. It's believed to be haunted. Many cliff divers have died there. Most of these cliff divers were non-Hawaiians or sailors. The falls drop 45 feet (13.7 m). There is a story that a god slipped and fell. This created the falls. The god lives at the bottom of the pool. The god wants sacrifices, or food. Cliff divers whose bodies didn't surface were believed to be taken by the god. The god would eventually release the bodies. The bodies would wash up to shore. In some photographs, people say they can see a ghost cliff diver. The ghost dives along with live cliff divers. At low tide, some people say they can see a skeleton shape. They believe the god is warning people to stay away. Cliff diving was banned. But today, professional cliff divers perform there.

Many cities and parks have banned cliff diving to protect their citizens.

dive off the 20-foot (6 m) cliffs. They splash into the rocky sea. A city official said, "If you don't know what you are doing, it's really dangerous." One cliff diver got knocked out. Another cliff diver was **paralyzed**. He couldn't move.

Many young people have died. Many parents are upset. They work with cities and parks. They want to ban cliff diving. The future of cliff diving is unknown. Cliff divers need to protect their sport. They need to be smart about being extreme!

Did You Know?

- Cliff divers can't dive for long periods of time. This puts a lot of stress on their bodies. They could shrink in height.
- Most cliff divers don't eat breakfast when they dive. It's harder to do twists on a full stomach.
- Orlando Duque once landed on a bird. The bird flew under him just as he hit the water.
- Many cliff divers hit jellyfish.
- Casa Bonita is a famous restaurant in Denver. It hires cliff divers. It has a 30-foot (9 m) waterfall. Cliff divers dive every 15 minutes for six hours. Families eat Mexican food while watching the divers.
- Justin Shiigi wears shark costumes when he dives off 50-foot (15 m) cliffs.
- Beginners should wear sneakers. Hitting the water feels like hitting concrete. Shoes help with the impact.
- Cliff divers swim and twist. This keeps them from being pulled in by the water currents.
- Justin Bieber went cliff diving. He burst his eardrum.

Consider This!

TAKE A POSITION! Guinness World Records no longer tracks cliff diving. They think it's too dangerous. They don't want to support cliff diving. Why do you think this is the case? Do you agree or disagree with their position? Argue your point with reasons and evidence.

SAY WHAT? The Nailed It! Series from 45th Parallel Press features books about BASE jumping, rock climbing, and cave diving. Compare cliff diving to these other sports. Explain their differences and similarities.

THINK ABOUT IT! Have you heard the phrase, "If your friends jumped off a cliff, would you?" Some parents feel that peer pressure causes teenagers to jump off cliffs before they're trained and ready. What do you think about this?

SEE A DIFFERENT SIDE! Why do you think cities and parks are worried about cliff diving? Why do you think parents are worried about cliff diving?

Learn More: Resources

PRIMARY SOURCES

9 Dives: A Journey Through Body and Mind (2005): www.9dives-the-movie.com.

SECONDARY SOURCES

Hamilton, S. L. *Diving*. Minneapolis: ABDO Publishing, 2015.

Labrecque, Ellen. *Cliff Diving*. Mankato, MN: Child's World, 2012.

WEB SITES

Red Bull Cliff Diving World Series: www.redbullcliffdiving.com

World High Diving Federation: www.whdf.com

Glossary

aerial (AIR-ee-uhl) happening in the air

currents (KUR-uhnts) strong flows of water

daredevil (DAIR-dev-uhl) person who does daring stunts

drag (DRAG) pulling force, resistance

impact (IM-pakt) to hit something hard

murky (MUR-kee) unclear

obstacles (AHB-stuh-kuhlz) objects that get in the way

paralyzed (PAR-uh-lized) unable to move

platform (PLAT-form) a board built for diving off of

polluted (puh-LOOT-id) poisonous

precision (prih-SIZH-uhn) accuracy

sacred (SAY-krid) special, holy

somersault (SUHM-ur-sawlt) a flip

takeoff (TAYK-awf) jumping-off point

tombstone (TOOM-stone) large, flat stone marking a grave

Index